A tale of Moominvalley

PUFFIN BOOKS

UK | USA | Canada | Ireland | Australia | India | New Zealand | South Africa

Puffin Books is part of the Penguin Random House group of companies
whose addresses can be found at global.penguinrandomhouse.com.

www.penguin.co.uk   www.puffin.co.uk   www.ladybird.co.uk

Penguin
Random House
UK

First published 2021
003

Characters and artwork are the original creation of Tove Jansson
Written by Richard Dungworth
Text and illustrations copyright © Moomin Characters™, 2021

Printed in China
A CIP catalogue record for this book is available from the British Library

PB: 978–0–241–48958–1

All correspondence to:
Puffin Books, Penguin Random House Children's
One Embassy Gardens, 8 Viaduct Gardens, London SW11 7BW

MIX
Paper | Supporting
responsible forestry
FSC® C018179

MOOMIN

and the
Midsummer
Mystery

BASED ON THE ORIGINAL STORIES BY

Tove Jansson

PUFFIN

In Moominvalley, it was one of those long, lazy midsummer afternoons. The Moomin family were all out of doors, enjoying the glorious weather.

Moomintroll's best friend, Snufkin,
was teaching him and Snorkmaiden
how to make a sound like a wild bird call –
by blowing across a thick blade of grass.
"Like this?" said Moomin, giving it a try.

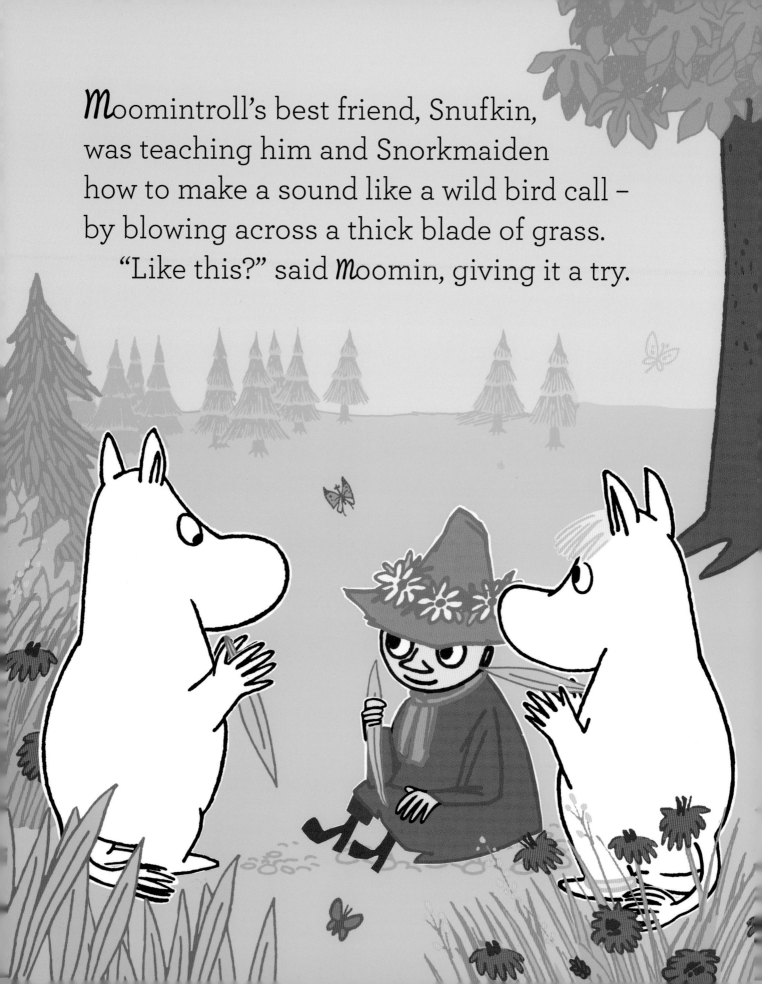

"Moominpappa, snoozing in the sunshine, stirred at the sound of Moomin's chirruping. "Gracious!" he declared, hurriedly rising from his hammock. "That's enough Serious Thinking for now. I must get back to work!"

He had spent much of the summer on his latest writing project. "A thrilling mystery story," he had told the family. "With a stolen jewel. And hidden clues. And disguises." There was only the final chapter still to finish.

As Moominpappa returned to the verandah, however, he made a shocking discovery.

"My writing notebook!" he cried, staring at the table. "And my best fountain pen! They've gone!"

"Are you quite sure that's where you left them, dearest?" asked Moominmamma gently. "As sure as the hair on my tail!" Moominpappa insisted. "They've been stolen!"

"Our very own mystery!" said Moomin excitedly – already he had made up his mind to solve it.

"We must search the scene of the crime!" said Moominpappa. "For clues."

But search as they might, they could find nothing out of the ordinary.

"Is it just me," said Snorkmaiden, "or does it feel cold here on the verandah? Even though the weather is so sunny!"

Moomin wasn't listening. He had just had an idea. He hurried inside the Moominhouse.

As he had hoped, Moomin found Thingumy and Bob upstairs, in the Room For Everything. The curious little pair, who loved collecting interesting things, were surely behind these strange goings on.

"A botenook and pountain fen?" said Thingumy, answering Moomin in the peculiar language he and Bob shared. "No, Troominmoll, we tidn't dake them." Bob, too, shook his head earnestly. "Treally ruly we didn't!"

Feeling rather disappointed, Moomin made his way back downstairs . . .

. . . to find that the mystery had taken another twist. "Someone put it back!" a bewildered Moominpappa told Moomin, waving his precious notebook. "While the rest of us were searching the garden for footprints. And look!"

The "someone" had written a single word,
rather messily, across a blank page of the book.
It read "LUNLY". This was not a word that
Moomin knew.

Snufkin, meanwhile, had made his own discovery. "Come and see," he told Moomin mysteriously.

One of Moominmamma's flowerbeds, behind the woodshed, was covered in frost. The ground was icy cold.

"Remember what Snorkmaiden said about the verandah being cold?" said Snufkin, giving his friend a dark look.

Moomintroll's tummy did a little flip.
"You . . . mean . . ."
Snufkin nodded gravely.

"It's the Groke.
She's been here."

The idea that the Groke – the silent, roaming stranger who froze all she touched – was behind the disappearance of Moominpappa's things caused everyone to panic.

Only Moominmamma kept calm. "She did put the notebook and pen back," she pointed out. She looked at her frozen flowers sadly. "And how awful. To be cold and alone on a day like this."
    This gave Moomin an idea.

Moomin considered the strange, scribbled word again – he realized that his mother was right. 'LUNLY' must mean 'lonely'. The Groke was very, very lonely.

Moomin remembered how lonely he felt sometimes when Snufkin went away for the winter. It was one of his least favourite feelings. "We should help her!" he decided bravely.

Moomin turned over the piece of paper with the Groke's sorrowful message and he wrote:

Dear Neighbour,

The Moomin family cordially invite you to an evening of storytelling tonight.

Then he put the invitation, with a plate of Moominmamma's home-baked biscuits, in the woodshed.

That balmy summer's evening, the whole family
gathered outside to hear Moominpappa read the
first gripping chapter of his finished story –
The Mystery of the King's Pearl.

As he listened, enthralled, Moomin could feel a welcome draft of cooler air coming from the nearby woodshed – and he was sure he caught a glimpse of the Groke. He hoped that listening to the story, in friendly company, would help the solitary Groke feel at least a little less "lunly".

When Moominpappa had finished reading – to great applause – Moomin made his way, rather nervously, to the woodshed.

"Mamma says," he called out bravely, "would you like to join us for supper?"

The Groke, however, had moved on, leaving only a patch of frost, a plate of biscuit crumbs . . .

. . . and beautiful, delicate ice crystals, which somehow remained frozen, even in the warm summer air.

"I think that's a 'thank you'," Moominmamma said, smiling.

After supper on the verandah, as darkness finally began to fall, Moomin settled down to camp out with Snufkin under the stars. "I think tomorrow I might try writing a story," he told his best friend sleepily.

"Mind you choose a nice big notebook," replied Snufkin wisely. "I have a feeling we're going to have lots of adventures worth retelling."

And Moomin felt quite sure he was right.

The End